MW00901740

GRANDMA BUFFALO, MAY, AND ME

By

CAROL CURTIS STILZ

Illustrated by

CONSTANCE R. BERGUM

SASQUATCH BOOKS
SEATTLE

ACKNOWLEDGMENTS

I am deeply grateful to my mother, Maybelle Fowlie Curtis, for sharing her stories of childhood in Polson and Kalispell, Montana. While May did catch fish, plant a garden, and feed buffalo in the early 1900s, this story is fiction.

Special thanks to the following for their contributions: Suzanne J. Curtis, who keeps our family stories and photographs; Kathleen and Kip Stilz, who supported my writing; Pacific Northwest Writers Conference for their recognition; Janet Asbury, Gene Barker, Margaret Barry, Donna Bergman, Beverly Porter, Peter Waugh, and Susan Yarger, gentle critics; Constance R. Bergum, imaginative illustrator; Lee Anne Martin, patient editor; Gary Hiam, my Montana guide; Edward S. Curtis, Henry Elwood, Paul Fugleberg, Jack Kehoe, Flathead and Mission Valley historians; Pat Jamieson at the National Bison Range, extension agent Jack Stivers, master gardener Jan Nutting, Kathy Bruno of International Apple Growers, Cheri Langoise and Germaine White, the staff at Timberland Regional Library, the Washington Department of Fish and Wildlife, and the Lake County Courthouse, for sharing information; George Beech and Rev. Russell Peck, fly fishers extraordinaire; Sylvia DeGooyer, Kip Stilz, Sharyl and Thomas Solberg, who drove the back roads of Big Sky country with me; and all people who work to bring back the American buffalo.

Text copyright ©1995 by Carol Curtis Stilz
Illustrations copyright ©1995 by Constance R. Bergum
All rights reserved.
No part of this book may be reproduced in any form
without the written permission of the publisher.

Printed in Hong Kong
Designed by Judythe Sieck

Library of Congress Cataloging in Publication Data
Stilz, Carol Curtis.
Grandma Buffalo, May, and me / Carol Curtis Stilz;
illustrated by Constance R. Bergum.
p. cm.
Summary: On her way to visit her grandmother in Montana,
a young girl learns more about May, the great-grandmother
whom she resembles, and meets a descendant
of the buffalo May used to feed.
ISBN 1-57061-015-0 : $14.95
(1. Great-grandmothers—Fiction. 2. Family—Fiction. 3. Bison—Fiction.)
I. Bergum, Constance Rummel, ill. II. Title.
PZ7.S86013Gr 1995
[E]—dc20 94-37220

Sasquatch Books
1008 Western Avenue
Seattle, Washington 98104
(206) 467-4300

To the land we call Montana,
its spirit and its people.
–C.C.S.

For my husband
and best friend, Ron.
–C.R.B.

As darkness crept over our campsite, Mama lit a lantern whose two tiny baskets made white light. I took Grandma's leather-covered photo album from our bag, opening it to our family tree.

Mama, Gray Bear, and I are going to visit my Montana grandma. Mama says we are on an adventure, creating a story for the branch that is ours.

"Mama, tell me again about our family tree."

"The roots of a family tree grow deep in time, Poppy. Each branch is a story of the people in our family who lived before us. Our album shows photographs of some relatives and tells part of their stories."

I named these relatives "the greats": great-grandparents, great-great-grandparents, and great-aunts and -uncles. They have old-fashioned names like Melvin, Harriet, Zillah, and Asahel.

I searched for a picture of May, who looked just like me. "Tell me again about Great-Grandma May."

"May was my grandmother," Mama said. "When she was young, her wavy hair was the color of poppies and her eyes were green as moss. Her laugh sounded like the spring we heard today bubbling from the earth. When May was your age, she learned to catch fish, plant a garden, and feed buffalo."

"Tell me again about the buffalo."

"My great-uncle told of a man named Samuel Walking Coyote, who brought buffalo to the Flathead and Mission valleys in Montana. Long ago, four baby buffalo followed him from the plains, where buffalo were hunted, to these valleys, where they were protected. The baby buffalo grew up and had calves of their own. The buffalo May fed were related to those baby buffalo."

"Will we see buffalo?"

"I hope so. Buffalo don't roam free now, but they aren't tame like cows. They're wild animals living in parks and on ranches. Some descendants of May's buffalo live near Grandma. They are probably fast asleep, and it's our bedtime too."

In the dark I listened for coyotes like those that sang May to sleep. I heard one call far away as I watched the moon rise. That night I dreamed of buffalo, May, and me in Montana.

The next morning we drove down the mountainside, stopping beside a stream.

Mama said, "Let's see if the fish are biting."

She tied a hook covered with soft fur to my line. The fur hid the hook and looked like the bugs on the water below. I held my new fly rod and Mama wrapped her hand around mine.

"Move your hand just past your shoulder, then bring your arm forward quickly."

On my first try, the hook caught on the bush behind me. On my second try, the line tangled in the grass. The third time, my line swished past my ear and my fly hit the water. Then Mama cast. Her line sang in the air before her fly touched the stream.

Suddenly I felt a tug.

Mama helped me reel in my line. A silvery fish flip-flopped from the end. I stroked its slippery body.

"Can we let it go? This fish is so big and sparkly!"

Mama slipped the fish off the hook. I helped her rock it gently back and forth underwater so it could breathe. It wiggled. When we opened our hands, it darted away.

After lunch we drove through wheat fields, past tall, round towers called silos. We drove down a dusty road toward a sign that read: Buffalo Bridge. I didn't see any buffalo. Neither did Gray Bear.

"Where are the buffalo?" I asked.

"Long ago, buffalo lived here," Mama said. "Now let's find May's place."

We stopped at a big, white farmhouse surrounded by poppies. We knocked on the door and introduced ourselves to the woman inside. Mama had written to ask if we could visit, explaining that May lived there when she was my age.

The woman smiled, gave me a sack, and said, "You're welcome to gather apples from May's McIntosh trees." We followed her out back.

Mama gave me a boost into a tree. Higher and higher
I climbed, under an umbrella of green leaves and red apples,
imagining May gathering apples too. I searched for buffalo
but didn't see any. Instead I saw faraway farmhouses, golden
grass, and a rainbow of flowers.

When I climbed down, the woman gave me two surprises. The first was a sealed envelope. She said, "I save the seeds from May's poppies. Plant them and next spring you'll have flowers the color of your hair."

The second surprise was a carefully wrapped twig. "This cutting from May's apple tree will root if you put it in rich soil. When its roots grow strong, plant it outside. With cuttings from May's trees, we grew the trees you see now."

"Thanks! Now I'll have my own little McIntosh tree."

"Perhaps someday your daughter will pick apples from your tree, and you can tell her the story of Great-Grandma May," Mama said. "Now let's find buffalo."

Back in the car, we drove along straight, dusty roads. I was hungry, so I took three apples from the sack. I gave one to Mama. Gray Bear wasn't hungry, so I stuffed his apple in my pocket.

I saw a sign that read: Buffalo Crossing.

"Are the buffalo here?" I asked.

"I hope so. Grandma knows the man who runs this ranch."

We stopped at a big log house, stepped up on the porch, and knocked on the door. The man who answered told us, "Buffalo are shy and stay away from folks they don't know. Still, you may see them on the hillsides, under trees, or near the river."

"My great-grandma May fed buffalo when she was my age, and I want to feed buffalo too."

The man's forehead wrinkled while he thought. "There is only one buffalo gentle enough to feed. Grandma Buffalo. She's my oldest, seventy-four in buffalo years. That's twenty of our years. I bottle-fed her as a baby, and she will eat from people's hands."

As Mama drove, she said, "Poppy, watch for buffalo."
"Look! Is that one?" I asked.

Our car inched along so we wouldn't scare the buffalo, but it moved farther and farther away until it disappeared. I searched the hillsides, watched the bushes, and stared into shadows beneath the trees. I didn't see any more buffalo, but I felt them staring at me.

"They must be hiding," I said.

Soon we would be leaving the ranch. I held my breath, hoping we would find Grandma Buffalo.

"Stop!" I shouted.

Mama parked our car. This buffalo was big and brown, with a hump and horns. We walked on short grass that crunched with every step. The buffalo ambled through long grass, quiet as a whisper.

We followed, strolling toward a woman waiting near the fence.

"Hi," she said. "I'm Mary Elizabeth Hawk. I visit Grandma Buffalo whenever I can. My family has raised buffalo since my ancestor Walking Coyote first brought them to this valley."

"I know about Walking Coyote," I said. "Are you related to him?"

"Yes, I am, just as Grandma Buffalo is related to the buffalo he brought with him."

"My great-grandma May fed buffalo when she was my age, and I want to feed buffalo too."

"Grandma Buffalo has four stomachs, so you won't spoil her appetite. She is very strong, but gentle."

I turned to Grandma Buffalo. A short, woolly coat covered her back. A shaggy mane covered her head and shoulders. Gray Bear thought Grandma Buffalo needed a haircut. I stroked her long, soft mane. Then I reached for Gray Bear's apple in my pocket.

"Grandma Buffalo, this apple is from Great-Grandma May's McIntosh tree."

Grandma Buffalo looked at me with big chocolate-drop eyes. She wrapped her long, purplish black tongue around the apple. Her tongue tickled. She rubbed her head against my hand, chewed, and swallowed. A soft sound in her throat said, "Thank you."

Mama laughed.

"She's talking to you, Poppy. Maybe her great-great-great-grandmother told her of a little girl with wavy hair the color of poppies who fed her apples long ago."

I gently patted Grandma Buffalo. "Do you remember?"

Later, Mama lit the lantern. She said, "Tomorrow night we'll see Grandma and sleep in her house."

I took Grandma's leather-covered photo album from our bag. Gray Bear and I turned its yellowed pages, searching for May's picture.

I imagined May feeding apples from her tree to a buffalo who lived long ago. I heard her buffalo rumble its thanks.

"Does Grandma know my story is like Great-Grandma May's?"

"What will you tell her?"

"Great-Grandma May and I shared an adventure. We learned to catch fish, plant a garden, and feed buffalo. Today I picked apples from her tree. Soon I will plant my twig and watch its roots grow strong. Someday I will pick apples from my McIntosh tree."

I touched the little branch of our family tree where my name was written. Then I said, "The roots of my family grow deep in time, just like Grandma Buffalo's."

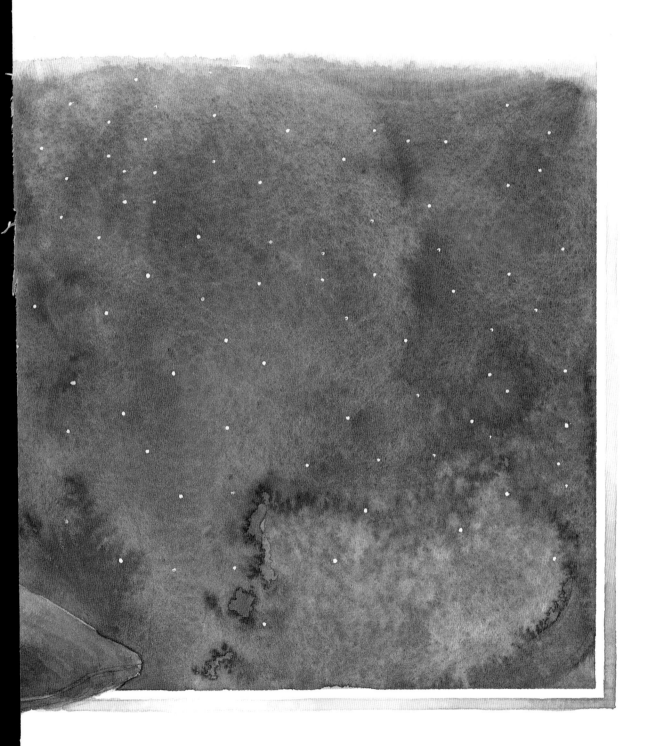